The Great, Great, Great Chicken War

Published by Anchorage Press, a division of Anchorage Foundation of Texas

Copyright ©2008 by David de la Garza, Joyce Rosner, and Gene de la Garza

All rights reserved under all copyright conventions.

For ordering information or special discounts for bulk purchases, please contact Greenleaf Book Group LP at: 4425 South Mo Pac Expwy., Suite 600, Austin, TX 78735, (512) 891-6100.

Design and composition by Greenleaf Book Group LP

Publisher's Cataloging-In-Publication Data
(Prepared by The Donohue Group, Inc.)

de la Garza, David.
   The great, great, great chicken war / David de la Garza ; with Joyce Rosner and Gene de la Garza. — 1st ed.

   p. : col. ill. ; cm.

   Summary: The tale of a conflict begun by those who are too afraid, or chicken, to address why they are fighting in the first place.
   ISBN: 978-0-9795266-0-2
   ISBN: 0-9795266-0-4

1. War—Juvenile fiction. 2. Fighting (Psychology)—Juvenile fiction. 3. Chickens—Juvenile fiction. 4. Stories in rhyme. 5. War—Fiction. 6. Fighting (Psychology)—Fiction. 7. Chickens—Fiction. I. Rosner, Joyce. II. de la Garza, Gene. III. Title.

PZ8.3 .D45 2007
[Fic]   2007928257

Printed in China on acid-free paper

10 09 08 07   10 9 8 7 6 5 4 3 2 1

First Edition

The Great, Great, Great Chicken War

David de la Garza

with

Joyce Rosner and Gene de la Garza

AnchoragePress

In the Great, Great, Great Chicken War,

The rooster rode the rhino out the door,
Angry and eager to settle a score.

Snakes joined the quest without asking why,
Hissing the rooster's shrill battle cry.

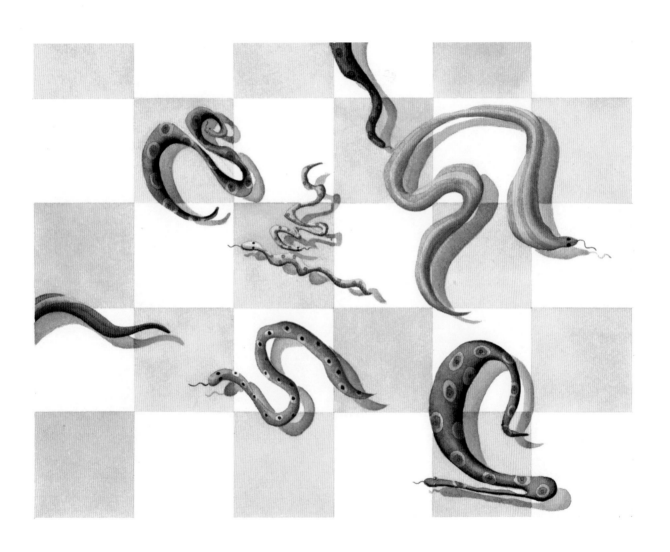

The world was confused, for the fight lacked reason.
Trees feared the worst, and bore fruit out of season.

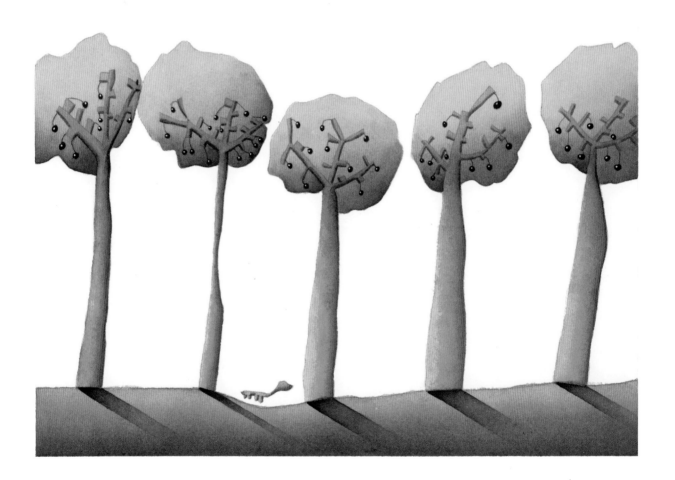

In the Great, Great, Great Chicken War,

Rockets filled the sky with a deafening roar,
Crisscrossing a land where peace was no more.

Velociraptors stormed across the isle,
Scorching the land for mile after mile.

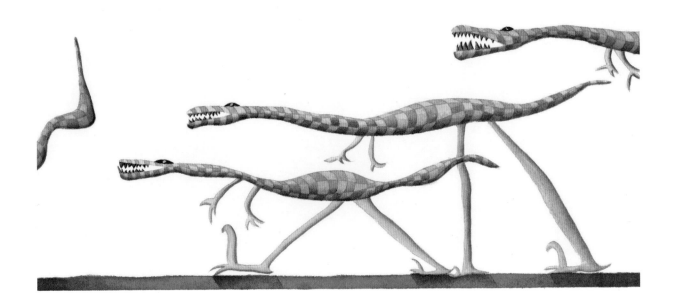

And in the deep ocean, where sea creatures sing,
Silent octopus feared what the future would bring.

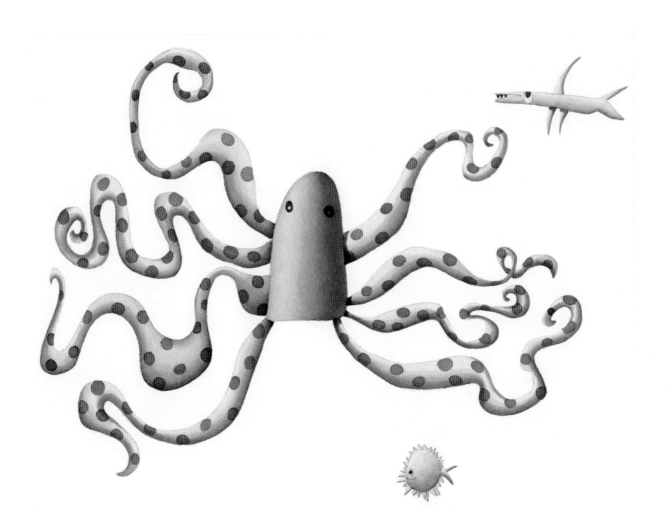

In the Great, Great, Great Chicken War,

The oceans seemed dark—not bright like before.
Could the animals ever be happy once more?

Then castaway pumpkins washed up on the sand,
Innocent victims in need of a hand.

So elephants, chickens, snakes, and the others
Gave the pumpkins great love,
Like sisters and brothers.

In the Great, Great, Great Chicken War,

Now-happy dragons broke rank by the score,
Ready to laugh and run and explore.

Monsters lost interest in fighting the fight;
The reason for fighting just didn't seem right.

So sea creatures cavorted and splashed with great cheer,
Welcoming fun times instead of more fear.

In the Great, Great, Great Chicken War,

Birds trilled in the trees a glad, "Nevermore!"

And the snails?
Now they feasted as much as they pleased,

On apples, corn, carrots, peppers, and peas.

So ended the Great, Great, Great Chicken War,
And the world found itself at peace once more.

This book began in 2003 as we struggled to explain the idea of war to our son David. He was just five years old, and had been hearing bits and pieces of news about the impending war in Iraq. Naturally, that led to questions. And naturally, we struggled to find answers that would tell him enough without telling too much.

We were living in Dresden, Germany, at the time, a city still emerging from the ravages of war and chaos left over from sixty years before. David had seen the damaged buildings that still stand there and understood a bit about conflict and fighting, of course. But his understanding was that of anyone whose life experience so far had been the cocoon of family, school, friends, and neighborhood. So our answer to his question was this: "War is the way grownups solve conflicts when they're too chicken to work out the real problems."

Our answer seemed to fit David's world—a place where he was advised to "use your words" to talk through problems and where being "chicken" instead of brave was without doubt a negative trait. But David knew there was more to all the talk of war than that. So he processed our explanation in his own way. David began to draw.

As with many children, drawing was a way for David to express his ideas and feelings at a very young age. His drawings from that time show the kind of directness and purpose that comes more easily to a child than an adult. And in this case, as he drew, he titled each drawing with what was later to become the first version of this book's text. That's when it became clear to us that he was working through all of this new information about the absurdity of fighting.

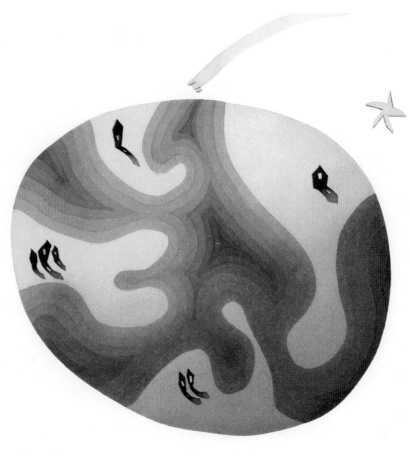

This book began in 2003 as we struggled to explain the idea of war to our son David. He was just five years old, and had been hearing bits and pieces of news about the impending war in Iraq. Naturally, that led to questions. And naturally, we struggled to find answers that would tell him enough without telling too much.

We were living in Dresden, Germany, at the time, a city still emerging from the ravages of war and chaos left over from sixty years before. David had seen the damaged buildings that still stand there and understood a bit about conflict and fighting, of course. But his understanding was that of anyone whose life experience so far had been the cocoon of family, school, friends, and neighborhood. So our answer to his question was this: "War is the way grownups solve conflicts when they're too chicken to work out the real problems."

Our answer seemed to fit David's world—a place where he was advised to "use your words" to talk through problems and where being "chicken" instead of brave was without doubt a negative trait. But David knew there was more to all the talk of war than that. So he processed our explanation in his own way. David began to draw.

As with many children, drawing was a way for David to express his ideas and feelings at a very young age. His drawings from that time show the kind of directness and purpose that comes more easily to a child than an adult. And in this case, as he drew, he titled each drawing with what was later to become the first version of this book's text. That's when it became clear to us that he was working through all of this new information about the absurdity of fighting.

We hope this book opens conversations between you and the children in your life as it has for us. We're glad you're reading it, and we hope you'll find a meaning here that fits your needs—whether it's a need to talk about a conflict at school or a need to fit the very big ideas of war into a package that tells your child what we tried to tell David: enough, but not too much.

If you're interested, we also invite you to share your thoughts and even your own text for this book at our website: www.castawaypumpkins.com— named for the pumpkins in the book, which to us represent children who are so often the victims of war. We've started the conversation with some alternate text of our own, developed during the very long process of turning those first drawings into the book that you hold in your hand.

Thanks for reading this, and thanks for being part of the conversation that grew into this book.

www.castawaypumpkins.com